But For Snow

AMY LAURENS

OTHER WORKS

Find other works by the author at
www.amylaurens.com

But For Snow

INKLET #45

AMY LAURENS

www.inkprintpress.com

Print ISBN: 978-1-925825-44-2
eBook ISBN: 9781393625087

www.inkprintpress.com

National Library of Australia Cataloguing-in-Publication Data
Laurens, Amy 1985 –
But For Snow
56 p.
ISBN: 978-1-925825-44-2
Inkprint Press, Canberra, Australia
1. Fiction—Fantasy—General 2. Fiction—Animals 3.
Fiction—Short Stories

First Print Edition: November 2020
Cover image © Sarah Richter via Pixabay
Cover design © Inkprint Press
Interior art © Amy Laurens

BUT FOR SNOW

THE MARKET IS TOO BRIGHT—TOO many people shouting, laughing, singing—and Tundra cringes, shrugging her shoulders up around her ears. The place is raucous; it makes her head hurt. The smell of cinnamon and hot oil smothers her nose from the food vendors' stalls, and the sunshine is fierce, making the damp ground humid and suffocating everyone with a hot, sapping afternoon.

Tundra wanders away a few steps, carefully eyeing her mother as she busies herself at a stall full of twisted metal jewellery. Tundra creeps a few steps more, the soft grass tussocks compressing under her feet as though they too are trying to be quiet in the hubub of the crowd.

She reaches the corner unnoticed, peeks back to see only her mother's fuchsia silk headscarf through the crush and bustle.

Tundra runs. If she runs fast enough, the people blur and even though it's noisy still, it's nearly as good as being alone. The rumble of the crowd is like the wind that whips her long hair and tickles her ears, and she laughs from deep in her belly because if she can just run fast enough, it's almost like flying.

Tundra pauses in the liminal space of a side-alley where the evening sun doesn't reach. She sobers; others give the alley a wide berth. Dark shadows clutch cages against the walls and the breeze that gusts from the bowels of the alley is cold and full of night, and the smell of old, dry things. Tundra peers warily, curiosity piqued by the multitude of eyes that reflect the dim light. She has always liked animals.

Tundra glances over her shoulder as goosebumps prickle her skin. Her heart hammers, not in fear of the inhuman night, but that someone might see her, might tell her she shouldn't be here. People are always telling her she shouldn't be in the places she wants to go.

The wind stirs her hair into wisps, ghost fingers teasing in the dark. Tundra tucks her hair firmly behind her ears and enters the alley, lungs filling with the dry-fur smell as she breathes deeply.

Iron-barred cages skulk in corners, and smaller wicker cages dance on ropes crisscrossing overhead, knocking hollowly in the breeze.

"Hello, pretty thing," Tundra says softly as she approaches the nearest cage, stretching out her fingers for its occupant to sniff.

The creature backs away and shivers, fur softly silver in the dim light, eyes wide and yellow.

Tundra holds the bars of the cage and wants to cry. Animal thoughts are not like human thoughts—they lack the words—but she can feel that the creature does not like its cage; it remembers skies, and treetops, and rain.

Something shrieks. Tundra whips around, adrenalin pulsing through her.

Perched on a cage above her head is a large, velvety black bird with snowy white chest feathers. Tundra moves closer, standing on tiptoes to see. The bird's beak is huge and it's so brightly coloured that Tundra wonders if someone has painted it. Then she sees the chain binding the bird's leg and her chest knots up again.

"I'm sorry," she whispers to the bird, bundling up her pity and sending it in a way the bird will understand. "My mother tries to keep me caged up too."

It isn't fair.

Something shifts in the crate below the bird and Tundra crouches. The crate is deep in shadow, and her eyes tell her it's empty, but she knows her eyes are wrong. She can feel the thoughts of the creature inside and watches carefully, waiting for the moment when it will reveal itself. "It's all right," she croons. "I won't hurt you."

There. A shadow darker than the rest, a hint of fur, a paw.

Tundra smiles. "See? That wasn't so hard." She kneels on the smooth-worn cobbles, waiting for the creature to throw off its shadow cloak entirely.

White fur catches the faint light. It is a wolf, half-grown, curled tightly nose to tail.

He opens his eyes, piercing Tundra with his ice-blue gaze.

She gasps, because deep within that gaze lies recognition.

He knows who she is.

She knows who *he* is.

And yet, of course, she doesn't.

He's only a wolf, with strange blue eyes and a cloak woven of darkness. But he *feels*… he feels like her dreams, the strange ones of ice and snow she's had as long as she can recall, the ones with a sense of something missing so strong it takes her breath away just remembering it.

The wolf cub looks like he would enjoy those dreams, Tundra thinks.

It's a simple enough matter to pick the cold iron lock with some splinters of wood and piece of wire off the ground, and although her heart hammers and her palms grow sweaty, no one approaches, no one asks her business.

After a minute or two, the door creaks open. The gangly cub stretches, undulating his back and ending with a shake of his tail. He yawns, twitches his black-tipped ears and stares up at her.

Her breath catches in her throat at the gaze of an apex predator—but he will not harm her, she thinks. He…

She swallows. He feels like the thing that has been missing from her dreams.

His tail wafts and his mouth opens in a grin.

Does he feel it too, the sense that this is a meeting long foretold? Only one way to know. Tundra walks away, glancing back at the cub.

He follows. Tundra breaks into a trot, then a run as she leaves the alley behind for the bright sunlight and warm smells of the streets. The cub keeps pace and together they run right to the edge of town, out to the plains of warm, sweet-smelling grasses—and somehow, this is how it's always been. But for want of snow, this could be her dreams come true.

The moon, full to bursting as it dips toward the horizon, reminds Tundra that her mother will be looking for her. She glances down at the wolf, unable to bear the thought of going home tonight without him. She's only just found him, the missing piece of her dreams.

And besides, she hates the house. It's not a special loathing, just dis-comfort born of a preference for soli-tude, for cold, for wide-open spaces.

The wolf stares up at Tundra and her breath catches in her throat. She reaches out and touches him for the first time. His fur, white but for his silvery-grey back and black-tipped ears, is cold. Tundra's heart leaps and she grins, half mad with the thought of her own cold wolf. His fur burns her fingertips like ice and she luxuriates, sinking her fingers right down to his skin.

The cub snaps playfully at the air and Tundra laughs, pouncing on him. They wrestle, growing careless, and Tundra suddenly feels his teeth. She freezes, stunned.

The cub whines and backs away, ears and tail low.

Tundra shakes her head. "It's okay," she murmurs, reaching out to him with her good hand—because the one he bit is not a good hand any longer: it's marked with a perfect row of round tooth-punctures, each one filled with ice. She rubs at them, but the ice will not melt. They look like a string of diamonds over the side of her hand.

The cub whines again and Tundra tussles his ears fiercely. "I like it," she insists, and he nuzzles his face against her as though he would lick her if he could.

Worn out, Tundra lies back in the grass and stares at stars that sparkle bright and brittle, promising winter. The cub curls up at her side and falls asleep, and although her mother will be furious, Tundra cannot bear to wake him.

Wrapped in cold and frost and the smell of fur, she falls asleep, and together they dream of ice and snow, and games played in the chilly breeze of death.

In the morning, the wolf cub is gone. The same sense of loss from her dreams floods over Tundra, and she lies still, her heart broken.

Mother. She will be livid. Tundra sighs and hauls herself to her feet— and the cub comes bounding to her side. He prances beside her, batting at butterflies, fur glistening in the early morning light.

Tundra grins, relieved. Mother won't let him stay with her at the house, but that doesn't matter. Tundra is an expert at hiding things from her family—and with six older siblings, that's no mean feat. But she takes the wolf to a pen of branches hidden in the forest behind the house in a thicket of boxalder, and feels confident that no one will come across him there.

Mother scolds her something fierce when Tundra creeps in the back door. Tundra cowers and makes innocent eyes at her, and Mother sighs in frustration. "Here," she says, handing Tundra a dishcloth. "You're on pots."

Tundra nods meekly and counts down the minutes as she spends her morning up to her elbows in the wreckage of her mother's latest canning spree.

It's lunchtime before she can escape back to her wolf, and as she nears the pen he howls. Tundra curls her fists, telling herself that her nails pressing into her palm are payment for the pain she hears in her wolf's cry.

Tundra's heart leaps when she sees the pen: the branches are turned to ice, and in one corner the wolf has nearly broken through.

She hesitates. Perhaps the wolf is not really hers, but wild. Perhaps she dreamed their bond. But one look in his eyes reassures her, and she sets about replacing ice with wood, crooning and soothing him as she works. He rubs against her and grins, tongue lolling to the side, and Tundra's shoulders lift. *See?* she tells her herself. *He is happy here.*

Once the pen is repaired, she pets him for a while, rubbing his ears between her fingers and scratching at the base of his tail. "I'll always come back," she tells him. "I promise. You mustn't fret while I'm gone. We're bonded now, and I must take care of you." She nods decisively. She will take care of him. She will.

Tundra trudges back to the house, where more chores await.

Snow-thoughts haunt the rest of her day.

At dusk she sneaks out again, and once more she must replace the walls of the pen.

The wolf is listless, but Tundra refuses to see that his eyes are duller, his gaze less piercing. She tussles his ears. "I can't sleep with you tonight, Snow Wolf. Mother will have my hide if I'm not in bed all night, and I know her: she'll come to check. But I'll be back as soon as I can in the morning. I promise."

The wolf whines as she hurries away, but she shakes her head and pre-tends it's nothing more than the wind whistling through the trees.

That night, for the first time since she can remember, Tundra does not dream of snow. She wakes with sandy eyes and a headache, feeling as she did the time her brother Thiel tricked her into drinking a large mug of Father's best ale. She drags herself out of bed and down to see the wolf, who stays curled in a corner of his pen and won't come near her, won't even stand.

Tundra's nails bite into her palms again. "I hate it just as much as you do," she mutters. "I'd much rather we could both roam free. But they'd kill you if they saw you. You're a wolf."

And Mother has told her on pain of bedroom imprisonment that she is not to wander off today, and because Tundra hates her room so much, she won't. "I'm sorry," she says to the wolf.

As she leaves, he howls.

Tundra spends the morning cramped in the confines of the laundry, chained to the washtub, scrubbing out clothes on the board.

By the time Mother calls her for lunch, her hands are wrinkled and pale as though they haven't seen the sun in days, and she feels about the same. The walls of the house close in on her and she feels irritable, like someone is watching her over her shoulder. But she slides her lunchmeat into her lap anyway, and bundles it up for the wolf.

Tundra dangles the meat over the edge of the pen, trying to entice the wolf. "Here, wolfie," she singsongs. "Nice wolfie." He ignores her.

Tundra throws the meat into the dirt and stomps away. "Stupid dog," she mutters.

She doesn't eat dinner that night, doesn't dream of snow.

"Chores today?" Tundra says over-brightly as she joins her mother in the kitchen.

Mother blinks in surprise. "If you like." She sets Tundra enough work to occupy her until the evening shadows begin to lengthen and the trees reach out to tangle their branches in the sun.

As Mother begins preparations for dinner, Thiel strides through the yard.

The movement catches Tundra's eye, and she glances up, only for the bottom to drop out of her world.

It's like she is falling, or drowning, or perhaps the walls are closing in and she is suffocating, because slung over her brother's left shoulder, perfect counterpoint to the rifle over his right, hangs a wolf, gangly and long-limbed like a half-grown cub.

It is only as Thiel has nearly disappeared that Tundra sees the wolf's eyes, glassy and staring, are yellow.

She drags in a shaky breath, removes her apron, and dashes through the yard. Fear and hope war in her chest, making it hard, so hard, to breathe.

At last she pushes into the thicket and the scene is exactly as she hoped—exactly as she feared: the wolf is curled in the same corner as always, his coat matted, his eyes dull.

The meat from yesterday still lies in the dust and ants busy themselves with devouring it. Tundra jumps the fence and kicks at the meat. "It's not your food!" she screams at the ants. "It's not for you!"

And she isn't quite sure if the last is directed at the ants, or the wolf—or herself. But the dreams. The dreams were real—weren't they?

The wolf still hasn't moved, and although she tries not to, Tundra thinks she can see his ribs. She throws the meat at him and storms away.

"Stupid wolf. Eat."

Tundra stomps into the house, ignoring as her father calls her to dinner. She is vaguely aware of her mother murmuring, but she doesn't really hear, doesn't really care.

In her room, she flings herself on the bed face down and drags a blanket over her head. Why won't the wolf eat? She *knows* it's hard being confined, but *she* does it, *she* tolerates it, because one day, she'll be old enough and she won't have to.

The wolf is just a baby still. They're meant to be together. How can they be together if he won't stay penned?

He can't die. He can't.

Tundra drifts off into an uneasy sleep, waking just as twilight fades. She stares at the darkening roof and sighs. She misses her dreams of snow.

Tundra hesitates at the doorjamb, staring out into the night. Her heart pounds and fear is eating her belly alive. *I don't want to,* she thinks. *I don't want to!* Eyes closed, she tries to feel the snow dream. Nothing but emptiness. She misses the dream so much it hurts, and that hurt is just a little bigger than the fear.

She grits her teeth. She must. Tundra pulls off the outer layers of her dress until she's in her shift and nothing more. This part wasn't planned, but as the breeze caresses her, raising goosebumps, she smiles grimly at the cold. Her body may protest, but the cold makes her alive; the cold is of the dream.

When she reaches the pen, Tundra doesn't look at the wolf. She doesn't want to see what might be reflected in his eyes—guilt, pity, or worse, nothing at all. Instead, she grabs the closest branch and tugs it away with an almighty crack. The sound is like her heartstrings snapping, and she claws at the fence in a fury. How dare they be contained. How dare they not roam free, she and her wolf. One day the world will pay for this imprison-ment. One day, there will be no fences that can stop them.

Before long, the gap is wide enough for the wolf to fit through. Tundra turns back to the house, still refusing to look, and walks away. If he's still there in the morning, well, then she'll do whatever might need to be done. But if he is anything like her, freedom hard won will restore his soul better than anymore assistance she could offer him.

A crackle of leaves as she nears the end of the thicket draws her involun-tary glance. It's the wolf, stepping gingerly out of the pen. His matted fur sheds before Tundra's eyes and new hair glistens in its place. The wolf whines once then leaps into the air, dancing. Tundra jumps too, breathing more easily than she has in days, and for a fleeting instant it could be her dream, but for the lack of snow. Then the wolf lands, whuffs, and lopes away. Tundra wipes the too-warm tears from her cheeks and closes her eyes, searching for the dream.

The wolf howls, and she sees it: she and her wolf, dancing with death in the soft-falling snow.

Tundra nods and, scrubbing at her cheeks, squares her shoulders. As she heads for the house, her wolf howls one last time, already far away, his voice as sharp and brittle as ice.

Tundra's vision is filled with a flurry of snowflakes that feather away all worries, all walls, all fences.

She smiles, chest light. One day, she and her wolf will dance again—and it will snow.

THE MAKING OF
BUT FOR SNOW

It's times like this I regret deleting all my old draft writing files. I thought, now that I use Scrivener to hold onto all my ideas and clips and draft files, that I wouldn't need all my old word docs of fifty-three billion draft versions of a story.

Little did I know that one day, I'd be pulling out these stories and writing commentaries on how and when and why I wrote them.

All of which is to say that I no longer have any record or idea of when I actually first wrote this story, although I think it was probably around 2010. Maybe 2009, when I was participating in a kind-of weekly short story challenge with some writer friends in an attempt to improve my short story writing skills.

Regardless, this story wins the prize for most heavily redrafted. I'm pretty sure it's gone through at least six or seven iterations, maybe more, whereas the rest of my short stories are usually in the two-to-three drafts realm.

Also, as you'll notice from the front cover, this story is part of the Kaditeos universe. I'm honestly not sure if it always was, or if it was co-opted in at a later point—there are no doubt things in here that are entirely anti-canon now—but regardless, this is Tundra, baby sister of Evil Overlord extraordinaire, Mercury, who is the main character of *How Not To Acquire A Castle* and sequels.

The tone of this story has always struck me as slightly formal, and a little distancing—but that's Tundra for you. If you read Mercury's books, you'll see Tundra there as a nearly-adult, still working to find her place in a world that doesn't appreciate neuro-divergence any more than ours does generally, still scrabbling for her identity and her place.

But regardless of how much of *But For Snow* may no longer be canon, there is always this: Tundra, and her wolf, and the future-dream that one day they will dance together again, and it will snow.

DOWNLOAD YOUR FREE EBOOK

When you buy a print book from Inkprint Press, we like to say THANK YOU by offering you the ebook for free!

Please head to www.inkprintpress.com/inklets/45/ and the use the coupon INK45 to get your copy of this Inklet in epub AND mobi today!
(Coupon will only work once.)

Read more by Amy Laurens!

HOW NOT TO ACQUIRE A CASTLE

CHAPTER ONE

On a hard plastic chair in the front row of the Great Hall in the world's fifth-best evil overlording academy, with its red-wooden parquetry floor that spoke of wealth and the beige, square panels of sound-boards speaking of conservatism on the walls, Mercury sat, pointedly not sweating.

Partly, this was because the Academy Administrators had deigned to turn on the air-conditioning earlier in the day, in recognition of the fact that the hall would be packed out with approximately six hundred bodies, all here to celebrate the graduation of about a third of that crowd.

But mostly, Mercury was pointedly not sweating because she made it a point never to sweat, sweat being an indication that she was working hard, and hard work being antithetical to her way of life.

However. If she *had* been sweating right now, it would not have been due to the uncomfortable warmth of six hundred packed bodies that even the air-conditioning system couldn't completely shift, or, in fact, from overexertion. Instead, it would have been caused by an even more unfamiliar concept in Mercury's emotional vocabulary: nervousness.

Mercury did not *get* nervous. Mercury got things *done*.

So the fact that she was sitting here, in the front row of the Great Hall, about to graduate from Evil Overlording Academy (with distinction), and was feeling *nervous*... She crumpled the black paper program in her pale fists. It made her furious, that's what it did.

Abjectly furious, that snooty-tooty Deviran with his stupid morals and his stupid I-don't-want-to-be-here and his stupid Overlords-are-empty-figureheads and his stupid face sitting ten people over, looking implacable with his deep brown skin and barely-there, precision-groomed beard, as though he knew it gave him a stupid air of alluringly stupid mystery…

Mercury scowled and searched for the train of thought that had been derailed, yet again, by Deviran's stupidity.

Ah. Yes. She was angry because she was nervous because she wasn't absolutely entirely one hundred and fifty percent sure that she'd beaten Deviran in their final exams, and 1) being anything less than a hundred and fifty percent certain of anything made her cranky, and 2) being beaten by Deviran for dux of the year would be utterly unbearable. She flicked away a piece of fluff that had become snagged under her immaculately magenta-painted nails and smoothed out the black paper program.

In the front corner of the hall, the starkly-attired string quartet with their traditional black instruments began playing the March of the Oncoming Doom. The screechy scrapes of hundreds of chairs on the hall's wooden floor sounded as the crowd climbed to its collective feet.

Mercury sat with her arms firmly folded for a few moments longer, until her best friend Sparky kicked her in the ankle.

"Get up, idiot," Sparky hissed, hints of real flame flickering through her flame-coloured pixie cut.

"No," Mercury said, flouncing to her feet and tossing her own glossy brown hair back over her shoulders. Four years she'd been playing by the Academy's rules in order to get what she wanted, and she'd had just about enough. Other people's rules should only be applied to plebs too stupid to invent their own.

Sparky rolled her eyes somewhere over Mercury's head before focusing on the stage, where the ceremonial party had begun entering.

Mercury clenched her jaw and narrowed her own eyes as the teachers of the Evil Overlording Academy filed onto the stage, dressed in their formal finery. Each teacher had their own distinctive look that matched their personality and their Overlording style, from severe charcoal suits to jet-black leathers, pastel ball-gowns and gem-toned lingerie and eye-blinding spandex, and even on one tiny old woman at the back, worn jeans and a grey flannel shirt. She was the one to watch out for, of course; Mercury could respect an Overlord who was confident enough in their abilities that they didn't need to telegraph them. It wasn't a look *she* would consider, of course, but still. She could respect it.

The band's march finished and, after a moderately awkward pause, the crowd sat. The Principal, pale skin and dark hair matching his suspiciously vampiric red-and-black suit, took the podium, and Mercury narrowed her eyes. He was doing a superb job of hiding his emotions—he was a premier Evil Overlord, after all—but she was Mercury, and unlike anyone else, she had the benefit of being able to rummage through people's consciousnesses. She was better at adding things *into* people's minds than taking information out, but he was telegraphing fear loudly enough that she could sense it without trying overly much.

Mercury pursed her lips.

Hmm.

The Principal cleared his throat at the blackened-wood podium, and the fear made it into his usually-unreadable eyes. "Before we begin," he said, and Mercury's stomach did a peculiar kind of flip-flop. "I have a pressing announcement to make regarding the safety of our students and their families."

He cleared his throat again and took out a sheet of paper from his pocket, unfolding it carefully and smooth-ing out the creases before beginning again. "The Council"—quiet booing echoed around the hall, and Mercury tsked impatiently— "have asked me to recommend that stu-dents from Tumul Tuos seriously consider postponing their return to town for a few days. The city is dealing with a *situation* at present which may present a danger to our students' health and safety."

Mercury's hands fisted at her sides and she forced herself to remain seated. What was wrong with her city? What had the Council mucked up now? A risk to the students' safety? There had to be more he wasn't telling them. Gently, Mercury tugged on his consciousness, implanting the suggestion that it might be better to share the news than to keep it secret. After all, how could they fight an enemy they didn't know?

"There are, ah…" He trailed off, glancing side to side as though wondering why his mouth had decided to continue.

Mercury didn't snicker, but she did press her lips together in satisfaction.

The Principal took a deep, steadying breath and seemed to change tack. "There has been one death already. The family have already been notified, so it is with much regret that I must inform you that Woovermyer will no longer be with us at the Evil Overlording Academy."

Murmurs broke out around the room, not all of them sad—to be expected in a school devoted to raising the next generation of dictators (ish) and despots (of sorts).

Mercury, however, crushed her program in her left hand, fist so tight her nails bit her palm.

"You okay?" Sparky murmured, leaning towards her.

Mercury gave a single, tense shake of her head and stared at the podium. Dead. Livie Woovermyer was dead in *her city*. And the Council hadn't done anything to stop it. Couldn't do anything to stop it, probably, given they'd warned the students to stay away. Livie hadn't been the strongest candidate in the year level, but she was no lightweight, either. It would take a lot of power to kill a Seven.

Enough was enough. A good thing Mercury was about to graduate at the top of the class, giving her the right to knock the lowest ranking current Overlord off their perch. Tumul Tuos would be hers in a matter of hours. And then there'd be no more of these wasteful deaths. Her city would be safe at last.

Madame Pompadour was up the front now, elbow gloves the same glimmery silver colour as her elaborate, piled-curls wig, eyelids gleaming with matching silver eye shadow, and abruptly Mercury realised Madame was there to make the announcement that would change her life forever. She leaned forward in her seat, ready to stand when her name was called.

"And now the announcement you've all been dying for," the Political Alliances teacher trilled, the frills on her evening gown fluttering as she moved. "The dux of this year's cohort!"

Sweat slicked Mercury's palms. Irritated, she reached over and wiped them on Sparky's thigh.

Sparky pushed Mercury's hands back into her own personal space bubble and Mercury, nervous to the edge of distraction, let her.

"Will you please join me in welcoming to the stage, our wonderful dux for this year, Deviran Goodsmith!"

Mercury froze halfway to standing. "Did she just say Deviran?" she whispered furiously to Sparky.

Sparky hauled her forcibly back down into her seat. "Yes," she hissed back. "Sit down, you're making a fool of yourself."

Mercury's spine snapped upright as she sat, and she arranged the folds of her long black skirt demurely. "No I'm not." She closed her eyes. "Deviran's going up to the stage, isn't he?" Even at a whisper, the misery in her voice was clear, but this time, she didn't care.

Sparky reached over and squeezed her hand.

Mercury squeezed back, lacing her fingers through Sparky's, and held tight as all her plans and dreams vanished in front of her.

A stone had landed in her chest. That must be it. Some strange sort of magic that made her chest contract and sink, and made the world distort for just a moment, long enough to trick her into thinking Deviran had beaten her so that someone could jump in front of her and yell SURPRISE!

Any moment now.

Any moment.

She refused to open her eyes and watch Deviran parading across the stupid stage like some stupid stupid-person, receiving his stupid medal and stupid symbolic crest pin.

It was that last exam question. She'd known Deviran would pull out his ridiculous 'Evil Overlords are merely figureheads, the Business Guild is where the power really lies' rant that everyone had heard a million times back when he was younger and angrier, and she'd tried to counter it, she really had.

She'd argued for the importance of the Overlording position, for the power of having a symbolic figure to unite the population in their hatred, for having a person able to make all the difficult, necessary decisions the Council was too weak and spineless to make... But it hadn't been enough. Everything she'd worked for, everything she'd set out to prove—and it wasn't enough.

There were words, there were names, and then forever later, once she'd died twice already, Sparky elbowed her in the ribs. "Come on," Sparky muttered. "We're up next."

And sure enough, there was a shuffling of presenters as the last of the Powers Behind The Thone graduates departed the stage, and the next speaker announced in threatening, funereal tones, "The Over-lording cohort."

Mercury blinked furiously and followed Sparky to the end of the line at the right side of the stage. The other candidates proceeded one at a time across the stage, two girls and then stupid Deviran, and then a handful more and then Sparky, and then the speaker was calling her name.

Hands fisted, Mercury tossed her head high, climbed the four steps, and marched across the stage. She wouldn't look at them, the stupid faculty who'd denied her the city she rightfully deserved, and she wouldn't look the other way either, at the classmates and crowd undoubtedly sniggering at her failure.

She shook hands with the presenter, and while he pinned the tiny crossed-swords badge on her collar, her eyes betrayed her and slid towards the aud-ience. Her stomach flipped as she saw the crowd of parents and friends behind the rows of students, all the way to the back of the hall, twenty rows at least, illuminated by the late afternoon light streaming in through the ceiling-high windows to the right. Everyone had someone here to watch them graduate. Everyone except Weird Al—and her.

The presenter finished with her pin, muttered something to her, and offered his hand again. Mercury coldly ignored it and strode from the stage. It didn't matter. None of it mattered. Tumul Tuos was her city anyway, and no one could change that. She'd think of something. She'd take a day or two out, make some plans...

And she could always hope that Deviran would choose some other Overlording territory. He'd be stupid to, but then again, he was stupid, so. Mercury could hope.

All at once, mid-way down the steps off the stage, Mercury came to rigid attention, scanning the room. Somewhere out there in the crowd, an exchange of power had just taken place, and it felt... unusual.

But the final few students were backing up behind her and muttering, so Mercury headed back toward her seat, craning her head all the while and searching for some sign of whatever it was that had just discharged a dizzyingly quiet amount of power into the room.

She sat, and Sparky leaned over. "Okay?"

"Mm," said Mercury. "Did you feel…" She accidentally caught the eye of the student behind her and twisted back to face the front.

"Feel what?"

Mercury turned it over in her mind. It had felt like a large shot of power discharged very quietly—but perhaps it hadn't been. Perhaps it had only been a small discharge after all, something most people wouldn't have noticed.

But still, something about it had tugged on her. It very nearly felt like something she'd felt before, only she *knew* she'd never sensed that kind of discharge before.

She shook her head. "Never mind. Don't worry."

Sparky sighed and straightened. "It's fine, Mercury," she said, drily exasperated.

"I know you didn't win, but I promise, you'll live through it."

Mercury waved a hand for silence.

The power had just discharged again, and it had come from somewhere in the back corner, far away from the windows and light.

Impatiently, Mercury waited for the formalities to conclude. The crowd stood while the quartet played the exit march, and the stage party left, Mercury tapping her foot all the while.

The moment the last notes of the march died away, Mercury turned and headed to the back corner, weaving in and out of the students and parents who had seemed to explode slowly but inexorably out from the neat rows of seating, ignoring Sparky's calls behind her. Power, something that tugged in a way that was strange and familiar, all at once. She pushed her way through a family posing for pictures—and halted.

In the shadows of the back corner, Deviran stood with his family, with his stupid, smug little smile, looking as tall and dark and stupidly alluring as ever. Prat.

His mother, short but sleek, and his father—tall, and utterly terrifying in a way not at all diminished by his gleaming smile—gushed over him, patting his back and hugging him tight. Within moments the Principal was there, glibly shaking hands and congratulating them on the success of their son. Something flickered across his consciousness, and also Deviran's father's—some moment of recognition in response to what they were saying.

But Mercury brushed it aside just as the mother brushed melodramatic tears from her cheeks and handed Deviran a silver-wrapped package about as long as her hand but half the width.

That. That was the source of the strange, magical feeling. Mercury watched hawk-eyed as Deviran un-wrapped the gift. A glimpse of gold set her pulse racing—What was it? What did it do? Could she steal it?—and then the paper fell away to the floor, and Deviran stood staring wordlessly at the object in his hands, and Mercury did too.

Wide-eyed, Deviran raised his gaze to his parents, and even from where she stood Mercury could hear the reverence in his voice as he thanked them.

But Mercury had eyes only for the object. No wonder she'd felt it discharge, and no wonder it had felt both strange and familiar. In Deviran's hands lay a glorious, sunshine-gold key, large and strong—and with a handle in the shape of a stylised fish, long, flowing fins curving to make the grip.

A Key. They'd given him a Key. And not just any Key, but *the* Key, *her* Key, the Artefact of Power belonging to *her* city.

A wordless noise of wanting rose in Mercury's throat. Who cared about being dux? She needed that Key.

Keep reading! Head to
https://www.amylaurens.com/books/
kaditeos/castle
to buy your copy now!

ABOUT THE AUTHOR

AMY LAURENS is an Australian author of fantasy fiction for all ages. Magical human-animal bonds have always been one of her favourite things about the fantasy genre. As well as this story, she wrote about them in the humorous fantasy *Kaditeos* series, following newly-graduated Evil Overlord Mercury as she attempts to acquire a castle.

She's also written about *non-*magical human-animal bonds in the *Sanctuary* series about Edge, a 13-year-old girl forced to move to a small country town because of witness protection, and about humans who turn into animals in the young adult *Storm Foxes* series.

INKLET
#031
Welcome
to Dark Dale
LIANA BROOKS

When War
Came to Town
A Powers Story
AMY LAURENS

Not
Fantasy
AMY LAURENS

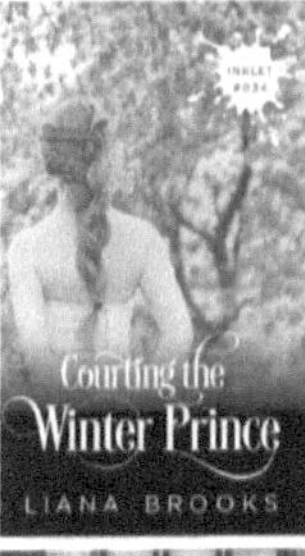
INKLET
#034
Courting the
Winter Prince
LIANA BROOKS

INKLET
#035
At the Home of the
Winter King
A Stone Faces Story
AMY LAURENS

INKLET
#036
With
This Ring
AMY LAURENS

DOUBLE ISSUE
Venus &
Seven Reasons I Said No
LIANA BROOKS

INKLET
#038
OATH KEEPER
AMY LAURENS

INKLET
#039
FORGET
A Powers Story
AMY LAURENS

INKLET #040
NOT QUITE
Cinderella
LIANA BROOKS

INKLET #041
ONE BAD MAN
AMY LAURENS

DOUBLE ISSUE
INKLET #042
The Claustrophobia
Of Loneliness &
Adam, Be A Star
AMY LAURENS

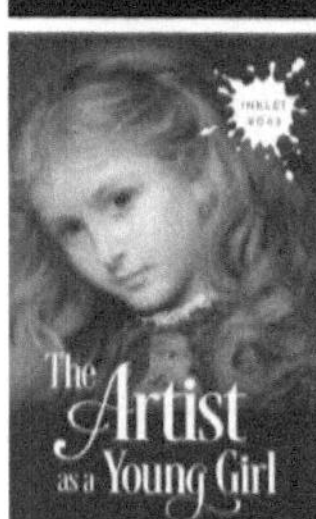
INKLET #043
The Artist
as a Young Girl
LIANA BROOKS

INKLET #044
CONFESSIONS
AMY LAURENS

INKLET #045
But For Snow
A Kaditeus Story
AMY LAURENS

INKLET #046
The Boy
Named NO
LIANA BROOKS

INKLET #047
Anamata
AMY LAURENS

INKLET #048
A Wolf FOR
Christmas
AMY LAURENS